You Choose Stories: Justice League
is published by Stone Arch Books,
A Capstone Imprint
1710 Roe Crest Drive
North Mankato, Minnesota 56003
www.mycapstone.com

Copyright © 2018 DC Comics.
JUSTICE LEAGUE and all related
characters and elements are © & ™
DC Comics. (s18)

STAR40192

Cataloging-in-Publication Data is available
on the Library of Congress website.
ISBN: 978-1-4965-6554-9 (library binding)
ISBN: 978-1-4965-6558-7 (paperback)
ISBN: 978-1-4965-6562-4 (eBook)

Summary: Black Manta has opened an
interdimensional portal, and now monsters are
spilling out into the sky, land, and sea! With
your help, can the Justice League stop the
ghoulish threat and seal *The Portal of Doom*?

Printed in Canada.
PA020

DC SUPER HEROES

←YOU CHOOSE→

JUSTICE LEAGUE™

## THE PORTAL of DOOM

written by
Laurie S. Sutton

illustrated by
Erik Doescher

STONE ARCH BOOKS
a capstone imprint

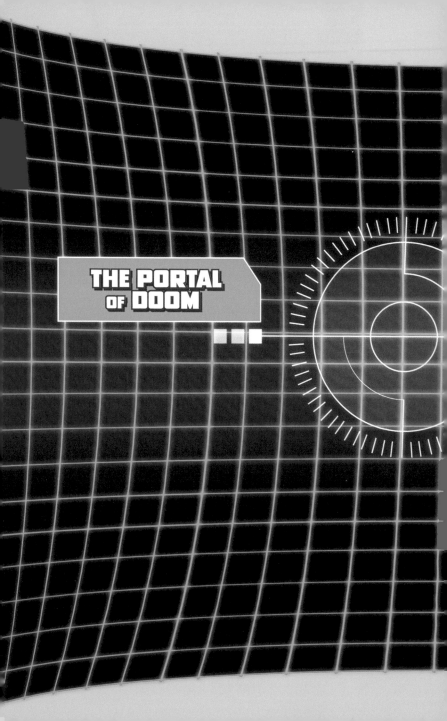

THE PORTAL
OF DOOM

On a small island, super-villain and treasure hunter Black Manta has uncovered an ancient artifact. But this is no ordinary antique—it unleashes monsters into the sky, land, and sea! Only YOU can help the Justice League defeat this ghoulish threat and close *The Portal of Doom*.

Follow the directions at the bottom of each page. The choices YOU make will change the outcome of the story. After you finish one path, go back and read the others for more Justice League adventures!

The super-villain Black Manta stands on the rim of an active volcano.

He looks down at the crater through the large red lenses of his helmet. All he can see is steam, but he knows molten magma lies beyond.

And below that is a treasure—a treasure that has been buried in the volcanic mountain on this island for thousands of years.

Black Manta fires energy beams from his eye lenses. They strike the inside of the volcano's crater.

**BAWHOOOOM!**

The rock explodes. Super-hot steam gushes from the opening.

Black Manta knows it won't be long before the volcano erupts with lava. He needs to get what he came for—and fast.

"Stand guard!" Black Manta orders his minions. Then he leaps into the boiling clouds of steam.

Turn the page.

Black Manta blasts through the rock and tunnels down through the volcanic mountain.

According to legends, ten thousand years ago this volcano was on the continent of Atlantis. A powerful Atlantean artifact was tossed into the molten core to keep it out of human hands. But after Atlantis sank, the peak of the volcano remained above the sea.

Black Manta wants to find the artifact.

"Uh, boss, things are starting to erupt up here," one of Black Manta's henchmen reports over the helmet comm.

Black Manta does not reply. He's focused on finding the artifact. He hopes that it will destroy his archenemy, Aquaman!

"Aquaman is from Atlantis, and only something from Atlantis will defeat him," Black Manta mutters.

As Manta's men guard the top of the volcano, lava starts to pour out from its side. Molten streams rush toward the small town below.

The town's mayor sends a distress call.
He knows there's only one force on Earth that
can stop a volcano. They need the Justice League!

* * *

Aboard the Watchtower—the Justice League's
headquarters that orbits above Earth—super hero
Black Canary sits at monitor duty. She sees the
distress call and quickly sends out a signal to
the League members closest to the emergency.

Superman, Batman, Wonder Woman,
Aquaman, Cyborg, Hawkgirl, The Flash, Green
Lantern, and Martian Manhunter respond
immediately. The heroes are on the way!

Aquaman is the first to arrive on the scene
of the disaster. He leaps out of the ocean and
onto the shore. He barely avoids the lava pouring
into the waters.

"This volcano hasn't erupted in decades.
What set it off?" Aquaman wonders. Then he sees
ten henchmen dressed in black armor, standing
on its rim. The answer is clear. "Black Manta!"

**Turn the page.**

Aquaman uses his sea-strengthened muscles to jump up the side of the mountain. He smashes into Manta's minions. Then the Sea King swings his trident.

**WHOMP! WHOMP! WHOMP!**

One by one, the criminals tumble down the side of the volcano. Soon there is no one left in Aquaman's way.

"Now, where's their boss?" Aquaman says. He looks down into the steaming crater. "Hmm. They were guarding this rim for a reason."

The Sea King leaps into the volcano. He plunges through the tunnel Black Manta blasted.

Aquaman lands in a big cave with a **THUMP!**

Black Manta spins around in surprise. Behind the villain is a gold tablet half-buried in an ancient, cooled wall of lava.

"You're too late, Aquaman! I have the instrument of your doom!" Black Manta declares.

The villain turns and fires his eye beams at the rock. The tablet drops to the ground. Black Manta expects the tablet to activate or show its power. But nothing happens.

"Well, that's disappointing," Aquaman says.

Furious, Black Manta tries to destroy the tablet. He fires another blast straight at the artifact.

A blaze of light suddenly bursts out of it—and so does a horde of monsters!

"It's an interdimensional portal!" Aquaman and Black Manta realize at the same time. They both dive for the tablet.

But monsters are swarming out of the portal. They carry Aquaman, Black Manta, and the tablet up and out of the volcano.

Aquaman grabs onto a huge, winged lizard monster. It soars high into the air. But then it turns sharply, and the hero loses his grip. Aquaman tumbles through the sky.

**Turn the page.**

"I've got you!" Cyborg says as he snatches the Sea King in midair.

The Justice League has arrived!

Superman digs a trench to direct flowing lava away from the town. Hawkgirl, Martian Manhunter, and Green Lantern fight the flying beasts. The Flash and Wonder Woman battle the land creatures. But many monsters spread across the land, through the skies, and into the sea.

"Where's Black Manta?" Aquaman shouts. "If he has the portal tablet, who knows what else he could unleash! We have to find him, and the tablet."

"No, we've got to defeat these monsters!" Hawkgirl says.

"I have a plan," Batman says as he lands his Batplane and joins his teammates. "We split up into teams and do all three."

To follow team Superman, Cyborg, and Hawkgirl, turn to page 13.

To follow team Aquaman, Green Lantern, and Martian Manhunter, turn to page 14.

To follow team Batman, Wonder Woman, and The Flash, turn to page 16.

"Superman, Cyborg, and Hawkgirl are the best at midair combat," Batman says. "You three team up to fight the flying monsters."

"And find that tablet!" Aquaman insists. "It can send the creatures back where they came from."

Superman zooms into the sky. Hawkgirl flaps her wings and follows right behind.

"Hey! Wait for me!" Cyborg says. The half-man, half-machine hero fires an extra boost from his boot jets.

The trio soars high above the island as the monsters fly off in every direction. In the distance, Cyborg spots something with his enhanced robotic eye.

"I see Black Manta's ship!" Cyborg says. "I'll go after him."

"No! We need you to help fight the monsters!" Hawkgirl exclaims.

Cyborg must decide what to do.

If Cyborg goes after Black Manta, turn to page 18.
If Cyborg stays to battle the monsters, turn to page 25.

"I can lead an underwater team, Batman. I choose Green Lantern and Martian Manhunter," Aquaman says.

Batman nods. "I agree. That's the best group for ocean combat. Green Lantern's power ring will protect him from the undersea environment, and Martian Manhunter can phase his body to let the water pass through his physical form."

"I can also shape-shift into any sea creature," Martian Manhunter reminds them.

"Let's go, team!" Aquaman says. He uses his super-strong sea muscles to jump from the base of the volcano and into the ocean a mile away.

"Someone is eager to get started," Green Lantern says.

He activates his power ring with his thoughts. The ring surrounds him with emerald-green energy, and he flies after the Sea King. Manhunter lifts into the air and follows behind.

The super heroes soar out to sea, and then dive below its surface.

As they swim below the waves, a pod of dolphins comes up alongside the heroes. They squeal and chatter at the Sea King.

"My finny friends tell me a terrible creature is attacking a nearby ship," Aquaman says over the comm unit in their belts.

"I can see a telepathic image of the scene in their minds," Martian Manhunter adds. "It's not just any ship. It's Black Manta's ship."

When the trio arrives, they see the Manta Ship in its underwater submarine form. An enormous octopus-like beast has its tentacles wrapped around the sub. They also see the super-villain swimming away with the tablet.

"I can stop Black Manta with my optic energy blasts," Martian Manhunter says.

"Wait! An optic blast opened the tablet in the first place," Aquaman warns. "If you accidentally hit it, you may free more creatures."

"What if I use my power ring?" Green Lantern asks. "Its energy isn't optic."

If Martian Manhunter fires his optic blasts, turn to page 21.
If Green Lantern uses his power ring, turn to page 27.

"Wonder Woman and Flash, you're with me," Batman says. "We have to stop these land monsters from harming the people on the island."

As the rest of the Justice League heads off to fight, the three teammates spot two groups of creatures. One lumbers toward a tourist town at the base of the volcano. The other slithers in the direction of a seaside harbor.

"Flash, wrap up the creatures heading for town. Wonder Woman and I will tackle the others before they get to the harbor," Batman says.

The Flash zips off in a blur of super-speed. Wonder Woman grips her golden lasso and leaps toward the harbor.

As Batman climbs into the Batplane, he sees a huge whirlwind form around the monsters near the town. It's The Flash running in circles. He's moving so fast that he creates a tornado.

The whirlwind lifts the monsters off the ground before they can reach the town. The Scarlet Speedster keeps running in circles to maintain the tornado. He moves back toward the mountain.

"I'm going to put these beasties back in the volcano's crater. It'll hold them like a corral," The Flash tells his teammates over the comm device in his belt.

### RUUUUMBLE!

The Flash never gets to the crater. Suddenly the ground shakes violently.

### BLAAAAM!

The volcano erupts and lava spews out from its top. The earth continues to tremble.

"Whoa!" The Flash cries, as he's thrown off his stride.

The hero's tornado falters. The monsters drop out of the swirling winds and rush straight toward the harbor.

Batman watches The Flash's creature chaos from the Batplane. That's when he also sees Black Manta's Manta Ship escaping.

Batman narrows his eyes. He must make a decision.

If Batman goes after Black Manta, turn to page 23.
If Batman stays to help save the island, turn to page 29.

"I can't let Black Manta escape," Cyborg tells his teammates and zooms away.

Cyborg chases the villain's manta-shaped aircraft through the sky. It fires missiles at the hero. But he dodges them easily.

"Ha!" Cyborg laughs. "Is that all you've got?"

Suddenly an alarm goes off in his internal radar system. Cyborg glances back. The missiles have turned around and are rocketing straight at him.

They're tracking weapons, and they're locked on Cyborg!

"Those things are stubborn," he mutters.

As the hero flies backward, he transforms his robot arm into his trusty sonic cannon. He fires.

### *BAWOOOM! BAWOOOM!*

Two of the missiles blow up. Cyborg is about to destroy the other two, but then he sees something.

The first two missiles have released a set of small bombs. They're hurtling toward him.

## *BOOOM! BOOOOM!*

The little airborne bombs are quick and strike Cyborg before he can react. The hero is rocked by the explosions. His cybernetic systems flicker on and off. He plunges toward the ocean below. The two remaining missiles follow him down.

*I'm not taking a swim today*, Cyborg thinks as he reboots his jets. He swoops back into the sky.

The missiles curve upward, still tracking him. This gives the hero an idea.

Cyborg heads at full speed toward the fleeing Manta Ship. He lands on the hull. The missiles fly right for him—and the villain's aircraft.

"How about a game of chicken?" Cyborg says.

The missiles continue to zoom ahead. Cyborg grows nervous as the explosive weapons get closer and closer. Is Black Manta really going to let the missiles hit his own ship? Was this the right choice?

If Cyborg jumps off the Manta Ship, turn to page 32.
If Cyborg stays put, turn to page 48.

"I am confident in my aim. I can hit Black Manta and not the tablet," Martian Manhunter tells his teammates.

**ZZZZZZT!**

A beam of energy shoots from his eyes.

At the same time, the monster lashes out. Its tentacle grabs the Justice League members just as Martian Manhunter fires his optic blast. The sudden movement knocks off the hero's aim.

The beams miss Black Manta and strike the tablet. It erupts with brilliant light.

"Uh-oh," Green Lantern says. He quickly forms a sphere of green energy around his friends.

When the bright light fades, they aren't underwater anymore. An alien landscape surrounds them. The Manta Ship lies nearby on its back. Beneath it, the octopus monster flails its tentacles. Black Manta is missing.

"We must've gone through the tablet portal," Aquaman realizes. "We're on the monsters' home planet!"

Turn the page.

Green Lantern lowers his energy sphere. Martian Manhunter flies into the alien sky.

"I will search for Black Manta," Manhunter says. "I will report back soon."

As Martian Manhunter soars away, Aquaman and Green Lantern walk over to the creature trapped under the Manta Ship.

"At least we got one monster back to where it came from," Green Lantern says.

"I am not a monster," the being says.

The octopus head shimmers and transforms into the clear dome of a helmet. The teammates are surprised to see an alien face inside.

"Then who are you?" Aquaman asks. "Why did you attack us?"

"Get this ship off me, and I will answer your questions," the alien says.

"Should we trust her?" Green Lantern whispers to Aquaman.

If Aquaman and Green Lantern decide the alien is friendly, turn to page 34.

If they decide the alien is a threat, turn to page 52.

Batman watches as the Manta Ship lifts into the air. He knows the craft has the ability to switch to submarine mode. It could dive underwater and disappear at any moment.

This may be the Justice League's best chance to capture the villain and the portal tablet. He can't pass it up.

"I've spotted Black Manta. I'm going after him," Batman tells his teammates over the comm.

The Dark Knight flies the Batplane around the erupting volcano. He knows the smoke and ash will hide him from the Manta Ship's sensors.

But the Batplane's tech is more advanced. Its enhanced radar can pick up the Manta Ship through the smoke. Batman grips the controls and speeds toward the villain's craft. A computer display puts it in a set of crosshairs.

Batman presses a button on the control panel. Two powerful Bat-Grapnels shoot forward.

**KTHUUUNK! KTHUUUNK!**

**Turn the page.**

The gadgets grip the villain's ship. Batman pulls up on the Batplane's controls. The Manta Ship comes along for the ride.

* * *

Inside the ship, Black Manta and his minions tumble across the flight deck. The villain clutches the Atlantean tablet to his chest. Then he uses his helmet's eye beams to slice through the hull.

The Manta Ship cracks open like an egg.

* * *

In the Batplane, Batman watches Manta's men fall toward the ocean below. He also sees Black Manta activating a jet pack, preparing to flee.

Batman gets ready to fire a net from the belly of the Batplane. He knows he can catch the henchmen. But if he tries to get Black Manta at the same time, he could miss the other criminals. He must decide if he should take that chance.

If Batman launches the net at Manta's men, turn to page 36.
If Batman tries to capture both Black Manta and his minions, turn to page 55.

Cyborg turns back toward the fight.

He doesn't like seeing Black Manta escape, but hundreds of enormous creatures are flying away from the island. The people of Earth have no defense against such a danger except for the Justice League.

"Let's swat these things!" Cyborg shouts.

**WHAAAP!**

A giant wing suddenly strikes the robotic super hero from behind. He tumbles toward the ground.

**WHOOOSH!**

A super-strong gust of air lifts up Cyborg as Superman blows a blast of his super-breath.

"Thanks, pal!" Cyborg says as he recovers his balance. Then he fires his boot jets and rejoins the battle in the sky.

**Turn the page.**

"Remember to keep an eye out for that tablet," Superman says as the three teammates continue to fight off the flying beasts.

"I see something!" Hawkgirl shouts.

She points to a lizard monster. It has the golden tablet in its claws.

"You have the eyesight of a hawk!" Cyborg says.

"Get ready to catch it," Superman says. He shoots beams of heat-vision at the creature's claws.

The beast screeches and drops the tablet. Hawkgirl swoops over and grabs the artifact.

"How is this thing going to stop the monsters?" Hawkgirl asks.

"Aquaman knows what it is. Take it to him," Superman replies as he wrestles four sky monsters. "Cyborg and I can hold off these creatures."

Hawkgirl hesitates. How can she leave her teammates in the middle of combat?

If Hawkgirl stays to fight, turn to page 69.
If Hawkgirl listens to Superman and leaves, turn to page 86.

"Your power ring might be the safest option, Green Lantern," Aquaman decides. "Just don't hit the tablet."

"No problem," Green Lantern replies.

Green Lantern imagines the shape of a giant hand. His power ring forms his thought into emerald energy. The hand reaches out and grabs Black Manta. The energy construct surrounds the super-villain—except the arm holding the tablet. It sticks out from between the giant green fingers.

Martian Manhunter moves his semi-phased body through the water like a ghost. He solidifies his fingers to snatch the tablet.

"Got it," Manhunter says.

Suddenly a swarm of monsters rushes up from the dark depths. They look like enormous worms with hard spikes covering their bodies. The monsters curl up and spin like buzz saws. They twirl straight toward the octopus, but the creature quickly swims away from the new foes.

So, the worms attack the Manta Ship instead.

**Turn the page.**

The ship breaks apart as the worm creatures buzz into it. Black Manta's minions spill out. Their uniforms and helmets protect them underwater, but they're not safe from the monsters' attack. The Justice League teammates race to the rescue.

Aquaman knocks the worms away with his trident. He uses his telepathy to call dolphins for help. Green Lantern whacks the creatures with the giant green fist holding Black Manta.

Martian Manhunter uses his shape-shifting powers to transform into a huge monster from his ancient Martian culture. His fingers turn to giant claws. But he loses his grip on the portal tablet! It starts to sink.

"Sorry. I will retrieve the tablet," Martian Manhunter says.

"Let it go!" Aquaman shouts. "We need your help rescuing the bad guys."

Manhunter hesitates. The tablet could send the monsters back. Can they afford to lose it?

If Martian Manhunter dives after the tablet, turn to page 71.
If Martian Manhunter stays to help his teammates, turn to page 89.

The Batplane hovers in the air. To the west, Batman sees the Manta Ship flying away from the island. To the east, he watches a horde of monsters lumber toward the harbor. Wonder Woman has her hands full battling the giant lizard creatures that are already there. Now, more beasts are about to arrive.

And the erupting volcano only adds to the chaos.

*I have to stay,* Batman thinks. *I have to help my teammates save the island.*

The Dark Knight is choosing to give up his opportunity to capture Black Manta. But he knows other members of the Justice League might have a chance.

"Black Manta is heading west in the Manta Ship. Be on the lookout," Batman tells his teammates on his belt comm.

He is certain one of them will catch the villain.

**Turn the page.**

As Batman turns the Batplane toward the harbor to help Wonder Woman, he gets a call on his comm device. It's The Flash.

"Batman! Things aren't good down here. The volcano is throwing out huge boulders. Plus, a lava flow is rushing down the side of the volcano, and it's heading for a nearby town," the speedster says. "I'm going to try to stop it, but I may need your help."

Before the Dark Knight can reply, he gets another call. It's Wonder Woman.

"Batman! A second wave of monsters is invading the harbor. Some backup would be appreciated!" Wonder Woman says.

Batman knows he can't be in two places at once. He must decide whom to help first.

If Batman goes to help The Flash, turn to page 73.
If Batman goes to the aid of Wonder Woman, turn to page 93.

Cyborg watches the missiles speed toward him. He's astonished that Black Manta would let his ship be destroyed by his own weapons.

"Manta might be ready to go down with his ship, but I'm not," Cyborg says.

He leaps off the ship at the last moment. But it's one moment too late.

The missiles explode as they hit Cyborg and the Manta Ship. Everything goes black.

* * *

Aboard the Manta Ship, Black Manta struggles with the controls. The blast has damaged the ship's flight engines. The Manta Ship zooms toward the ocean surface, trailing smoke.

The large craft hits the water and immediately begins to sink.

Black Manta switches to a set of underwater engines. It's a good thing the Manta Ship is also a submarine.

## *PING! PING!*

The submarine's sonar picks up an object. Black Manta turns on the underwater cameras. Inside his helmet, the villain smiles at what he sees.

"Cyborg . . . unconscious and sinking like a lump of high-tech metal alloy," Black Manta says. He activates a grapnel arm on his ship. It snags Cyborg and starts pulling him in. "I want to study that alloy."

\* \* \*

A sharp jab wakes Cyborg.

"Ow!" the hero yells. Then he looks around.

Cyborg is in a cavern filled with scientific equipment. He's strapped onto an exam table. Lasers and drills point down at him.

Cyborg realizes where he is. It's Black Manta's secret base!

"Your alloy is extremely tough. No wonder you survived my Manta Missiles," Black Manta says.

**Turn to page 38.**

Aquaman and Green Lantern decide to take the chance that the alien is friendly.

In his mind, Green Lantern pictures a giant mechanical claw. His power ring transforms the mental image into the real thing, except made of emerald energy. The claw grips the Manta Ship and easily lifts it off the alien.

"Thank you. I am Officer Dilara, head of security on the prison planet Annris," the being says as she stands upright on her tentacles. She looms over the humans. "Back on Earth, I wasn't attacking you. I was trying to get the portal tablet. You got in the way."

"Then we're after the same thing," Aquaman says. "We were trying to get the tablet away from a criminal."

"Speaking of criminals, you said you came from a prison planet," Green Lantern says. "Is that where we are now?"

"Yes. But we are far from any of the prison buildings," Dilara replies.

"So, if this is a prison planet," Aquaman realizes, "that means all the creatures that came through the portal are criminals. We've got to get back to Earth!"

"We have to find that tablet first. It's a gateway to and from this world," Officer Dilara explains. "More prisoners could escape to your planet if it falls into the wrong hands."

"If we find Black Manta, we find the tablet," Aquaman says. He activates the Justice League comm in his belt. "Aquaman to Martian Manhunter. Report."

"I have Black Manta in sight, but there is a problem," Martian Manhunter replies.

"What sort of problem?" Aquaman asks.

"I've been captured by Black Manta," Martian Manhunter admits. "I—"

The comm suddenly cuts out.

Turn to page 42.

Batman launches the net straight at the falling henchmen. As the net wraps around them, Black Manta fires his jet pack and flies away.

But Batman isn't worried. The Batplane is faster than Black Manta's jet pack. He can catch the villain in no time.

The Dark Knight zooms after Black Manta and readies another Bat-Grapnel. He lines up the crosshairs of the launcher and centers the villain in his sights. Batman is about to launch it when Black Manta dives toward the ocean.

Batman tips the nose of the Batplane downward to follow. Under the aircraft, the henchmen moan as the net is dragged along.

Suddenly Black Manta disappears into the sea.

"He's wrong if he thinks he can escape underwater," Batman says as he pulls the ship up.

The Batplane can transform into a sub. But first Batman has to drop off Manta's minions. And he sees the perfect spot.

The Dark Knight swoops in a wide curve toward a nearby fishing boat. He hovers the Batplane over the deck and releases the net.

Black Manta's men fall into an open cargo hatch. They land right on top of a heap of fish. The fishermen slam the hatch shut and wave at Batman. The Dark Knight gives a nod and zooms away.

Batman presses a series of buttons on the aircraft's controls. The wings fold back, and an underwater engine powers up. The Batplane has transformed into the Bat-sub!

The Dark Knight tips the front toward the ocean and dives below the waves.

Black Manta is nowhere in sight, but Batman doesn't need to see. He can track the villain with sonar. Just like a bat.

**PIIING! PIIING!**

**Turn to page 45.**

"I'll show you how tough the rest of me is too," Cyborg says.

He sends all extra power to his arms. He pulls against the metal straps with his robotic strength.

**ZAAAP!**

Black Manta shoots a stun bolt from his wrist gauntlet. It hits Cyborg's bare shoulder, and a burst of electricity pulses through the hero. Cyborg falls weakly back onto the exam table.

"Your cybernetic half is powerful, but your human flesh is weak," Black Manta says.

Cyborg fights against the dizziness he feels after the stun bolt. He tries to mentally activate his sonic arm cannon or his finger laser. He tries to fire his boot jets. Nothing happens.

Then he sees his arm cannon and boot parts on a table nearby.

He is being disassembled!

"I don't have the Atlantean tablet, but I'll take your mechanical parts," Black Manta says. "Then I'll transform them into weapons that will defeat Aquaman and the Justice League!"

"Well, you missed one thing—my Justice League emergency signal," Cyborg says as he activates the device in his belt with a simple thought. "Thanks for giving up the location of your secret headquarters."

Black Manta stares at the hero for a second. Then he runs for the exit. He does not get far.

**CRRRAAASH!**

Superman arrives at super-speed and smashes through the ceiling of the lab. Hawkgirl is right behind him. Black Manta fires his eye beams and gauntlet bolts at the super heroes.

The beams bounce off Superman's chest. Hawkgirl swings her mace club and knocks the energy bolts back at Black Manta. The bolts hit the lab equipment. It starts to explode.

**BLAAM! BLAAAM!**

**Turn to page 41.**

Black Manta dodges the explosions and dashes toward the door. He uses his eye beams to cause more destruction as a distraction. Smoke and fire fill the lab.

"Nice try, Black Manta. But you can't escape my super-vision," Superman says as he scoops up the villain.

Hawkgirl bats her powerful wings. The gush of air sweeps away the smoke and puts out the fires.

"Um, can I get a little help here?" Cyborg says from the exam table.

Hawkgirl smashes the metal straps with her mace. She hands Cyborg his missing parts.

"Now that we've captured Black Manta, we can finish mopping up the monsters," she says.

Cyborg reattaches his boots and arm cannon.

"Well, I'm armed and ready. Let's get to it!" Cyborg declares and blasts off.

**THE END**

To follow another path, turn to page 12.

"We have to save Martian Manhunter!" Green Lantern exclaims.

"It's a trap. Black Manta will be expecting us," Aquaman says.

"Then we do the unexpected," Dilara suggests. "I have an idea."

* * *

Green Lantern zooms down out of the alien sky toward Black Manta. He shoots bursts from his power ring.

**BZZZOW! BZZZOW!**

Black Manta returns fire with his eye beams.

**ZAAAT! ZAAAT!**

While they fight, Aquaman runs up to a circle of bonfires. In the middle of the circle lies Martian Manhunter. Fire is the Martian's greatest weakness. It drains his strength and powers.

Aquaman isn't fond of fire either, but he leaps over the flames to free his teammate.

Martian Manhunter is barely conscious. Aquaman lifts him up and jumps out of the ring of fire. They land far from the flames, but not far enough to escape Black Manta's notice.

"You tried to distract me!" Black Manta says.

He fires another blast at Green Lantern. Then he quickly turns and launches mini-missiles from his wrist gauntlet. The explosives speed toward Aquaman and Martian Manhunter.

Aquaman bats away the missiles with his trident—right back at Black Manta!

The villain destroys the weapons with his eye beams before they hit him. The air fills with smoke. When it clears, Aquaman, Green Lantern, and Martian Manhunter are standing in front of him.

"We didn't *try* to distract you," Aquaman tells Black Manta. "We already did."

**WHAAAAP!**

Officer Dilara smacks the villain from behind with a gigantic tentacle.

**Turn the page.**

Black Manta hits the ground. He's out cold. Officer Dilara plucks the portal tablet from the villain's belt.

"Perfect," she says. "Now I can conquer Earth!"

"Wait, what?" Green Lantern asks.

The alien laughs. "You fools! I am no security officer. I am mighty Queen Zordo. It was *my* army that escaped through the portal. Now that I have the tablet, I will rejoin them. I will bring more troops. We will rule the galaxy!"

Queen Zordo wraps her tentacles around the tablet. "And you cannot stop me. For you are just three pathetic weaklings."

"You're wrong," Aquaman says.

The Sea King grips his trident. Green Lantern's power ring glows. Martian Manhunter rises into the air.

"We're the Justice League," Aquaman continues. "And we'll be taking that tablet back."

**THE END**

To follow another path, turn to page 12.

The Bat-sub's sonar soon picks up the shape of Black Manta moving fast under the water. He appears to be heading back toward the island.

The Dark Knight is about to use the Justice League comm to warn the authorities on shore. But then he sees another shape appear on the sonar screen.

It's huge, and it's moving straight for Black Manta.

"That's a sea monster!" the Dark Knight says.

He watches the sonar blip that represents the villain continue forward. Black Manta must not realize what's ahead of him.

Batman pushes the Bat-sub to full speed. Black Manta is rushing toward big trouble. The villain doesn't know it yet, but he's going to need the hero's help.

The Dark Knight watches the two underwater objects approach each other faster and faster.

**Turn the page.**

When he reaches the two signals, Batman switches on the Bat-sub's underwater spotlights. They reveal a shocking sight.

Black Manta struggles in the grip of a creature ten times the size of a human. Its body is like a horseshoe crab, but instead of legs it has tentacles with snapping claws at each end. Several of them are wrapped around Black Manta.

The villain shoots his eye beams at the creature's armored underbelly, but the monster doesn't even twitch. Instead it squeezes tighter.

Batman slows the Bat-sub and quickly studies the situation. The creature is too big for any Bat-Grapnel or net. The Dark Knight has a few mini torpedoes, but even Black Manta's powerful optic blasts didn't have any effect.

Batman frowns. He might not be able to save Black Manta—at least not alone.

"It's time to call in some backup," the Dark Knight says. He activates the Justice League comm device in his belt.

"Batman to Aquaman. I could use a little help at these underwater coordinates," he says. "And bring some of your finny friends."

In no time the Sea King rushes in with a fleet of sharks. Hammerheads bash into the monster like battering rams. Great whites chomp down on its tentacles. Aquaman uses his trident to pry Black Manta out of the sea monster's grip.

As soon as the super-villain is free, he uses his underwater jet pack to zoom away.

"Thanks for rescuing me, fools!" Black Manta says with a laugh.

### SNAAATCH!

A Bat-Grapnel grabs Black Manta. It reels the villain toward the Bat-sub. Black Manta slams up against the cockpit window.

Inside the Bat-sub, Batman cracks a small smile. "You're welcome."

### THE END

To follow another path, turn to page 12.

Cyborg tightens his grip as the missiles continue to rocket toward him and the aircraft. He's not jumping ship. His plan has to work.

Suddenly the Manta Ship drops out from under Cyborg's feet.

That's not part of the plan. The craft dives into the ocean. It's also a submarine!

Cyborg dodges the missiles at the last second. Then he activates his oxygen mask. It pops out of his robotic chest just as he plunges into the water after Black Manta.

The missiles try to follow Cyborg underwater, but they fizzle and sink. The hero doesn't watch them go down, so he doesn't see what comes up to eat them.

A giant sea monster swims up from the depths. It swallows the unexploded missiles like sardines. But the creature is still hungry.

It senses Cyborg's movements and goes after its next meal.

* * *

Cyborg's boot jets are powerful in the air, but the water slows him down. It's just enough for him to lose track of Black Manta. Disappointed, Cyborg heads toward the surface.

### *CHOMP!*

Something grabs Cyborg by the leg and pulls him back. He turns around in surprise.

"What in the—whoa!" Cyborg exclaims.

He is eyeball to eyeball with a creature that seems to be made entirely of gigantic fish scales and teeth.

That's all that Cyborg sees, or wants to see. He fires his boot jets. Cyborg blasts free from the beast's bite and rockets toward the surface.

Cyborg bursts up out of the ocean and gasps in relief. He hovers above the water.

"I am *not* going to be fish food!" Cyborg says.

Then the monster leaps out of the sea and swallows Cyborg in a single gulp!

**Turn the page.**

Cyborg tumbles down the throat of the sea monster. He can't tell which way is up or down. The giant, squishy tube pushes Cyborg down into the creature's stomach.

**SPLOOSH!**

At last, Cyborg drops into a large area covered in total, slimy darkness. The slime stings!

"Ow!" Cyborg complains as he wipes the goo off his bare skin. He uses his robotic infrared eye to see in the dark. He figures out what's causing the pain. "Digestive acid. Gross."

His infrared eye scan reveals something else. Two large metallic objects are also trapped in the wet slime of the monster's stomach.

"Those are Black Manta's missiles," Cyborg says. "They just might come in handy."

**Turn to page 59.**

Aquaman and Green Lantern are suspicious of the alien. The being flails her tentacles. She tries to grab one of them.

"Nope. She's definitely not friendly," Green Lantern says.

"I am Queen Zordo. I am the conqueror of vast territories, leader of vast armies!" the alien boasts from beneath the Manta Ship.

Aquaman and Green Lantern look around at the harsh, empty landscape. All they see are low hills covered with boulders and dead trees.

"These are some really nice 'vast territories' you've got," Green Lantern says.

"Yeah. And I'm not seeing any 'vast armies,'" Aquaman points out.

"Rude creatures. You will pay for your insults!" Zordo declares and squirms beneath the Manta Ship. Suddenly it rolls aside.

Zordo is free!

Zordo lashes out with her giant tentacles. Aquaman leaps into the air and uses his trident to swat away the alien limbs.

He lands on top of Zordo's dome helmet. He stomps with super-strong sea legs.

*THUUUMP!*

The blow knocks Zordo unconscious.

"Never mess with a Sea King," Green Lantern says, looking down at the defeated being. "Now let's find Martian Manhunter."

"Good idea," Aquaman agrees. "We should have heard from him by now."

Green Lantern uses his power ring to create an energy surfboard for Aquaman, and the teammates take off into the sky. In the distance, they spot Martian Manhunter's eye blasts. They quickly realize why he hasn't reported back.

Their friend is surrounded by a horde of monsters. Martian Manhunter is in the middle of a massive battle, and he's fighting for his life!

**Turn the page.**

"It looks like Zordo has vast armies after all," Aquaman says. "The portal must have transported some of them to Earth."

Green Lantern forms a pair of giant binoculars with his power ring to get a closer look. He and Aquaman look through the lenses.

They see hundreds of monsters clashing on the rocky shores of the alien seacoast. Land beasts battle sea creatures. Sky monsters swoop down and attack them both. Then they spot Martian Manhunter and Black Manta fighting back-to-back against the hordes.

"Well, that's something you don't see every day," Green Lantern says.

"Let's get down there," Aquaman says.

Green Lantern creates a sea wave of green energy, and Aquaman rides it on the surfboard toward the battle. The wave crashes against a group of reptile monsters.

"Wipe out!" Aquaman says as he leaps off the board and right into snarling wolf creatures.

Turn to page 62.

Batman makes a quick mental calculation. He's ninety percent sure he can catch all the criminals. He fires the net.

It snares Black Manta and the minions in midair. Even with his jet pack, the super-villain can't escape the tough webbing. He kicks and squirms as the Batplane heads back for land. The netted criminals are dragged along for the ride under the aircraft.

Black Manta grips the ancient tablet. "No one is going to stand in my way," he says. "I *will* use this tablet to destroy Aquaman!"

### ZZAAAAT!

Black Manta fires his optic blasts. They burn a hole in the net, and then slice right through the Batplane above. The aircraft splits in half, just like the Manta Ship.

The super-villain escapes through the hole and activates his jet pack. He flies away as the Batplane and his minions drop toward the sea.

**Turn the page.**

Black Manta never looks back, so he doesn't see Batman jump out of the Batplane and spread the wings of a large Bat-glider.

The Dark Knight swoops down after the falling henchmen. Manta's men are still tangled in the net. Batman reaches into his Utility Belt and pulls out a Batrope attached to a Batarang. He flings the Batarang with all his strength. It wraps around the netted criminals.

Batman pulls up on the glider just in time to save Black Manta's minions from hitting the ocean surface. He watches Black Manta jetting away.

The Dark Knight can't go after Black Manta while carrying the henchmen, but he doesn't have to. He activates the Justice League comm device on his belt.

"Batman calling Superman," he says. "I've spotted Black Manta at these coordinates. I have my hands full at the moment and could use some backup."

Turn to page 58.

## *WOOOSH!*

A few seconds later, the Man of Steel arrives. Black Manta squirms in the hero's firm grip.

"You really do have your hands full," Superman says as he sees Batman holding onto the net full of Manta's men. "Let me give you a lift back to the island."

Superman grabs the Bat-glider with his free hand and flies everyone back to the erupting island. They land in front of a police station in the tourist town.

As soon as their feet touch the ground, Superman takes away Black Manta's weapons. He removes the villain's helmet, jet pack, and gauntlets. Then he crushes them into a tiny metal ball.

Batman takes the tablet from the villain and slaps Bat-Cuffs on his wrists.

"I'll take care of the volcano while you put these villains behind bars," Superman tells Batman and leaps into the sky.

**Turn to page 65.**

Suddenly Cyborg falls back as the "ground" moves out from under him. He struggles against the churning waves of digestive fluids. The sea monster is swimming upward! Cyborg grabs onto one of the missiles like a rescue float.

**WOOOMP! WOOOMP!**

Cyborg feels the vibrations of distant explosions. A few moments later, he sees pieces of the Manta Ship slide into the monster's belly.

"Looks like I've got company in the stomach of doom," Cyborg says.

Black Manta scrambles out of the wreckage. The angry villain takes out his fury by wildly blasting everything with his powerful eye beams. He doesn't care what he hits.

The beams barely miss Cyborg and the missiles.

"Hey! Watch where you're shooting those things!" Cyborg yells.

**Turn the page.**

Black Manta ignores him and keeps firing. The creature's stomach starts to gurgle and heave. This gives Cyborg an idea.

The super hero picks up one of the missiles. He throws it, and it explodes against the beast's stomach wall. The sea monster's belly shakes.

"Hey!" Cyborg yells at Black Manta. "If we work together, we can get out of here. You use your eye beams, and I'll throw this last missile. We can make the monster throw up—and us with it."

Black Manta doesn't say anything. He just increases his blasts against the stomach.

"I'll take that as a yes," Cyborg says.

As Black Manta fires at the walls of the sea creature's stomach, Cyborg lifts up the second missile. He throws it with all his cybernetic strength.

**BLAAAAAM!**

The effect is immediate. The creature's stomach shudders. The juices start to swirl.

"This is going to be messy," Cyborg groans.

The sea monster leaps out of the ocean like a whale. It spews Cyborg and Black Manta out of its mouth and into the air.

As they arch through the sky, Cyborg fires his sonic cannon at Black Manta. The villain fires his eye beams. The blasts meet in the middle.

**BWAAAAAM!**

The explosion sends the two flying in opposite directions.

Cyborg hits the sea miles away. He scans the area for Black Manta, but the villain has disappeared.

Suddenly another sea monster rises up and gulps him down.

"Aww! Not again!" Cyborg exclaims.

**THE END**

**To follow another path, turn to page 12.**

Aquaman fights off the wolf creatures with his trident and sea-strength. They come at him four at a time. He defeats them four at a time.

Across the battlefield, Black Manta spots the bright orange scales of Aquaman's uniform. He immediately leaves Martian Manhunter to go after his archenemy.

### BZZZAAAAT! BLAAAAM!

Black Manta fires his eye beams. He pushes through the monster warzone toward Aquaman. When he finally reaches the Sea King, he laughs in triumph.

"I told you I had the instrument of your destruction!" Black Manta says. He holds up the portal tablet. "I doom you to stay here forever!"

The super-villain fires an eye blast at the tablet. He expects the energy to transport him back to Earth.

Nothing happens.

"It looks like we're doomed together," Aquaman says.

Black Manta throws the tablet at Aquaman and tries to run, but the hero knocks him to the ground with his trident. The wolf monsters snarl and move in to attack. But Aquaman puts his foot on the back of Black Manta and growls a single word.

"Mine."

The monsters back off.

"Like I said . . . don't mess with a Sea King," Green Lantern says as he and Martian Manhunter land nearby.

"Manhunter, your optic energies caused the tablet to transport us here. Maybe they'll return us to Earth," Aquaman says, holding out the tablet.

The Martian Manhunter takes the tablet and blasts it. Still nothing happens.

"Hmm, Manta's optic beams didn't work on it either," Aquaman says. "We may be stuck here."

Suddenly the teammates hear a tremendous roar rise up from the warring monsters. They all look toward the top of a hill.

**Turn the page.**

Queen Zordo stands on the hilltop. She waves her tentacles and then thunders toward the battle.

"Time for us to leave," Green Lantern says.

He forms a sphere around his friends and Black Manta. He launches up into the air, pulling the others along.

"You'll never get back to Earth without the portal tablet," Black Manta says.

"Then it's a good thing I come equipped for space travel," Green Lantern replies.

He forms a sleek spaceship with his power ring. Aquaman and Martian Manhunter sit down in comfy chairs. Black Manta sits in a jail cell. Green Lantern takes the controls.

"I recognize the star patterns. We're not too far from Earth," Green Lantern says.

"Then let's get home," Aquaman says, "and help the Justice League round up the rest of Zordo's vast army."

**THE END**

To follow another path, turn to page 12.

Batman folds the wings of the Bat-glider and takes Black Manta and his minions into the police station. It's empty, but Batman isn't surprised. Every police officer must be busy dealing with the chaos outside.

After he locks the criminals in jail cells, Batman studies the ancient tablet. The symbols are unlike anything he's ever seen.

"Aquaman called it a portal tablet," Batman mutters. "Is it responsible for starting this whole monster mess?"

Suddenly the Dark Knight hears Black Manta laughing.

"Ha ha ha! You'll never get it to work, Batman," the villain says from his cell. "My helmet blasts activated it, but Superman destroyed my helmet. Good luck putting those monsters back where they came from!"

"Thanks for the information," Batman replies. "Now all I have to do is create an energy that's the same as your helmet blast."

**Turn the page.**

## THUMP! THUMP!

The police station trembles as giant monsters lumber down the street outside. Batman knows he needs to hurry. He needs to find a way to re-create Black Manta's eye beams.

He searches the police station until he finds the forensics lab. It's filled with high-tech equipment for solving crimes.

"There have to be a few things in here I can use," Batman says. He begins picking up gear. "A power source here, a laser there, a magnifying lens or two . . ."

The Dark Knight uses his genius-level mechanical skills to build a small energy cannon. It looks like a box with a stubby tube on one side.

"It's not pretty, but it should do the trick," Batman says.

The hero runs out of the police building. He opens his Bat-glider. The sea breeze catches the wings and lifts him into the sky.

Batman soars above the town. He holds out the portal tablet with one hand. With the other, he activates the energy cannon.

**ZZAAAAT!**

The beam strikes the tablet, and a blaze of light erupts from it.

Batman drops the energy cannon and holds the tablet with both hands. His whole body shakes as monsters are sucked into the artifact. Creatures pour in from everywhere—land, sea, and sky!

"Uurrrgghhh!" Batman groans.

Suddenly Superman appears at the Dark Knight's side. Then so does Wonder Woman. Together the heroes grip the tablet.

A few minutes later the tablet shuts down. The light disappears. The monsters are gone.

"Great job, Batman!" Wonder Woman cheers.

"All in a day's work for the Justice League," Batman replies.

**THE END**

To follow another path, turn to page 12.

"I'm sorry, Superman," Hawkgirl says. "But I can't leave my teammates to fight without me."

She shoves the tablet into her belt and starts swinging her mace club.

**WHAAAAM!**

She strikes a powerful blow on the ribcage of a gigantic monster. The breath is knocked out of its lungs, and it wobbles in the air. The creatures might be big, but they have their weaknesses.

Like a bird of prey, Hawkgirl swoops around the creature's lizard head. She delivers a blow to its jaw.

**POWWW!**

The monster's eyes roll up as it loses consciousness. It falls through the sky like a rock—straight toward Cyborg!

But the hero's attention is on fighting another monster. He doesn't see the threat hurtling straight toward him.

"Cyborg!" Hawkgirl shouts. "Look out!"

**Turn the page.**

### *THWUMMP! THWUMMP!*

Cyborg fires his sonic cannon down at his foe. The powerful sound waves hit the creature like a hammer. But the sound also drowns out Hawkgirl's warning.

### *WHOMP!*

Suddenly something strikes Cyborg. He's knocked sideways and catches a glimpse of a huge object falling past him.

The shape plows into the sky monster Cyborg was fighting. Both figures tumble down through the air.

"Are you all right?" Hawkgirl asks as she hovers next to him.

Cyborg realizes that it was Hawkgirl who pushed him from danger's path. He looks down. The two creatures are sprawled on the ground.

"I'm feeling better than those monsters are right now," Cyborg replies.

**Turn to page 75.**

Martian Manhunter decides to retrieve the portal tablet. The tablet is the best way to get the monsters off Earth. He swims down into the depths. But the object is sinking faster than he thought!

*A normal Earth metal would not sink this quickly*, Manhunter thinks. *Which means the tablet is not from Earth. Where did it come from?*

Martian Manhunter wriggles his monster tail and swims faster. The deeper he goes, the darker it gets. Soon it is pitch black.

So Martian Manhunter is surprised to see lights sparkling in the distance.

*I'm not near the undersea city of Atlantis. What is that?* Manhunter wonders.

He puts his curiosity aside and finally catches up to the portal tablet. He grabs it and starts to swim back toward the surface.

But then he notices the lights have gotten closer.

**Turn the page.**

The small lights surround Martian Manhunter. They look like a swarm of undersea fireflies. The hero isn't worried. After all, he's in the form of a huge sea creature, and they're just tiny sparks.

But then the lights suddenly wrap around him and squeeze tightly. Manhunter realizes these aren't individual lights—they're glowing tentacles attached to a gigantic monster!

More tentacles whip out at him. A whole school of monsters grabs Martian Manhunter. He swivels his eyestalks and sees they look like glowing jellyfish with crab shells for armor.

"Uhhh," Manhunter groans. "Must . . . break . . . free."

He uses his shape-shifting power to change into a beast from Earth legend. Martian Manhunter is now a mighty kraken! He increases his size until he's three times as big as the attacking jellyfish monsters.

But they don't let go. Then even more come out of the dark depths!

Turn to page 79.

Suddenly Batman hears a choking sound over the comm.

"Batman! Toxic gas . . . help!" The Flash gasps.

"He's in danger!" Batman says. The situation makes his decision for him. "Wonder Woman, Flash needs help immediately. I'll come to you as soon as I can."

The Dark Knight swoops the Batplane toward the lava flow. He dodges boulders being thrown out by the erupting volcano. It's like flying through a meteor shower.

At last he spots The Flash's bright red uniform through the smoke and ash. It isn't moving. Batman realizes The Flash must have been knocked out by the toxic volcanic gas. Batman has to get him out of there—fast.

Soon Batman reaches The Flash. He sends out a Bat-Grapnel and snags his teammate.

**WHHHHOMP! WHHHHOMP!**

Heavy boulders suddenly drop right next to the Batplane.

**Turn the page.**

"Time to get out of here," Batman says.

The Dark Knight switches the Batplane back to normal flight mode and lifts into the air. The Flash dangles from the Bat-Grapnel below the aircraft. Rocks streak past the aircraft, but Batman can't make any sharp turns to dodge them. With The Flash still hanging underneath the Batplane, a sudden change in direction could put him in danger.

**WHAAAAAAM!**

Suddenly the Batplane tilts violently to one side. Alarms flash and beep on the control panels. As Batman struggles with the flight controls, he glances out the cockpit window.

One of the wings is missing!

"Hold on, Flash, we're going down," Batman says, even though he knows his friend can't hear him.

**Turn to page 82.**

Not far away from Hawkgirl and Cyborg, Superman slams into one of the flying monsters. He pushes it into another monster, and then another and another.

### THWUMP! THWUMP! THWUMP!

Soon he has a stack of creatures all piled up. Superman shoves them toward the ground.

The monsters fall on top of the creatures Cyborg and Hawkgirl have already defeated. Superman lands and uses his super-cold breath to freeze the air. A prison of ice forms around the beasts. Hawkgirl and Cyborg land next to Superman.

"Well, that's eight down and hundreds more to go," Hawkgirl says. "We have to do better than this."

"Aquaman said the tablet could send the monsters back where they came from," Cyborg says. "But how?"

"The tablet might give us a clue," Superman says. "Let me see it."

**Turn the page.**

Hawkgirl takes the artifact from her belt and hands it to her teammate.

"This writing looks like Atlantean," Superman says as he studies the half-melted markings.

"Can you read it?" Cyborg asks.

"It's badly scarred, but I can see past the damage," Superman replies as he scans the artifact with his microscopic vision.

"I can help with that," Cyborg says. He uses his cybernetic eye to examine the artifact.

"I can too," Hawkgirl adds. "I *do* have the eyesight of a hawk, after all."

"The script on the surface of the tablet is Atlantean," Superman says.

"But it's written over something else," Hawkgirl adds.

Cyborg frowns. "It's another language."

Superman concentrates all of his super-vision powers on the ruined symbols. "It's Kryptonian!" he says in surprise.

"Are these monsters from your home planet?" Cyborg exclaims.

"They don't have my superpowers, so probably not," says Superman. "Maybe the tablet is some Kryptonian tech that the Atlanteans found."

"Does the Kryptonian writing tell us how to use the tablet?" Hawkgirl asks.

"Yes," Superman replies. "Stand back."

Superman aims his heat-vision at the tablet. Instead of melting, the artifact absorbs the energy. It starts to glow.

A beam of light shoots out from the tablet. Superman aims the beam at the creatures in the ice prison. The light sucks them into the tablet.

"Booyah!" Cyborg cheers.

"It should be easy to clean up this monster mess now," Hawkgirl says.

"Eight down and hundreds more to go," Superman replies, and then launches into the air.

**THE END**

To follow another path, turn to page 12.

Martian Manhunter struggles against the horde of jellyfish monsters. Even his enormous size can't stop them. They swarm him like ants.

But he does not call for help from his Justice League teammates. He won't draw them away from their battle in the waters above. And he can't put them in danger by taking this fight to the surface.

So he's surprised when he sees Aquaman swoop out of the darkness. Behind him follows an army of tuna, swordfish, and sea turtles. They charge at the jellyfish creatures and start to chomp on them. Manhunter is able to break free.

"Jellyfish are the natural food for my finny friends. Even alien jellyfish," Aquaman explains.

"How did you know I was . . . having trouble?" Manhunter asks as he returns to his humanoid form. "I did not call for help."

Aquaman waves a hand toward an enormous shadow in the deep water. A magnificent whale glides into view.

**Turn the page.**

"One of my sea subjects saw you were in danger and told me," Aquaman explains.

"Thank you," Martian Manhunter replies and pats the gigantic finny friend.

"Come. Let's get topside," Aquaman says. Using his telepathy, he asks the whale to lift them toward the surface.

They arrive to floating wreckage. The sea monsters are gone, but the Manta Ship is scrap. Black Manta and his minions are behind prison bars formed of green power ring energy. Green Lantern sits on top, drumming his fingers.

"There you are!" Green Lantern shouts. He flies over.

"I have retrieved the tablet," Manhunter says.

"Now we just need to figure out how to put it in reverse," Aquaman says.

Green Lantern uses his ring for a low-energy scan of the tablet. The scan displays an image of the artifact's markings, but in a language the teammates understand.

"These markings show that the *strength* of the energy doesn't activate the tablet. The *frequency* does," Martian Manhunter says.

"Manta's eye blast must have hit just the right frequency to activate the portal," Aquaman adds.

"I can set my power ring to match the frequency. Then we can activate the portal and send the monsters back," Green Lantern says.

Martian Manhunter holds out the tablet, and Green Lantern strikes it with a beam of emerald energy. Brilliant light bursts out of the artifact.

Immediately all the monsters from the land, sky, and water are sucked back into the portal! When the creatures are gone, the portal automatically shuts down.

Aquaman takes the tablet from Martian Manhunter. "I'll bring this to Atlantis and lock it in an undersea vault," he says. "I'd say it's time to put it away for another ten thousand years."

**THE END**

To follow another path, turn to page 12.

The Batplane tips to one side and spins downward. Batman has no control. He can think of only one way to save The Flash and himself.

Batman watches the ground rushing toward him. He calculates the aircraft's rate of speed and starts a mental countdown.

At the last moment, the Dark Knight releases the Bat-Grapnel. The Flash falls away from the doomed Batplane. At the same time, Batman pops the cockpit dome and ejects from the aircraft.

Both teammates hit the ground and tumble. Three hundred feet away, so does the Batplane.

**CRAAAASH!**

Batman uses his acrobatic skills to roll and break his fall. He staggers to his feet and rushes over to The Flash.

The Dark Knight reaches into his Utility Belt and pulls out a miniature oxygen mask. He puts it over his teammate's face.

"Cough! Cough!" wheezes The Flash as his eyes open. "Ugh . . . what happened?"

The Flash notices the wrecked Batplane, and his eyes widen.

"I'll tell you later," Batman replies. "But it means that I can't deal with the volcano. It's a good thing I've thought of something else."

He describes his strategy. Then Batman hands The Flash a gas mask from his Utility Belt, just in case there's more toxic smoke.

"I like the way you think," The Flash says and zips away in a blur.

The Scarlet Speedster races toward the lava flow heading for the town. When he reaches it, he stomps on the ground with super-speed.

### *BOOM! BOOM! BOOM!*

The vibrations create a large crack in the earth. The lava pours into it. As The Flash super-stomps away from the town, he forms a path for the lava to flow down to the ocean.

The molten rock hisses and hardens as it hits the seawater. This gives The Flash an idea.

**Turn to page 85.**

He uses his super-speed to run across the surface of the ocean. Then he races around in a circle. The speed forms a swirling vortex. It lifts up water until it creates a waterspout.

The Flash guides the watery tornado back to shore and up the volcano. When he reaches the main source of the lava flow, the hero stops running and releases the waterspout. The water dumps onto the molten lava. It hardens and plugs the volcanic vent.

The Flash zooms back to where he left the Dark Knight. "The volcano is taken care—"

He stops talking. He finds Batman standing beside ten unconscious monsters. His empty Utility Belt lies on the ground.

"It turns out this wasn't a safe place to crash," Batman explains.

More growling creatures lumber toward them.

The Flash sighs. "Oh, right. The monsters. Back to work!"

**THE END**

To follow another path, turn to page 12.

Superman sees Hawkgirl hesitate. "Take the tablet to Aquaman!" he says. "Cyborg and I can handle things here."

Hawkgirl hates to leave a battle, but she listens to her teammate. She flies clear of the swarming sky monsters and activates the Justice League communication device in her belt.

"Hawkgirl calling Aquaman," she says. "I have the tablet."

"Excellent!" Aquaman replies over the comm. "We can use it to send these monsters back through the portal."

"I'll bring it to you. Where are you now?" Hawkgirl asks.

"I'm one hundred miles east of the island," Aquaman says. "I'm heading for an oil rig that's under attack."

"I'll meet you there," Hawkgirl promises.

As she flies away on her mission, she tells herself, *I'm not abandoning a battle, I'm just heading for a different one.*

Hawkgirl soars high above the waters at top speed. Soon she sees an oil rig. Giant eels slither up the sides. Crab-like creatures snap at the human workers who are trying to defend themselves with welding torches and wrenches.

Hawkgirl grips her mace club. It crackles with energy. She dives out of the sky.

Hawkgirl smashes her weapon against the hard shells of the giant beasts. The creatures shudder, but they don't stop their attack.

"These things are tough," Hawkgirl says. "But I'm tougher."

Hawkgirl swoops around the monsters. She puts all her strength behind each blow of the battle mace.

### *CRUUNCH!*

The crabs start to crack.

### *BLORRRMF! BWOMFFF!*

The soft bodies of the giant eels wobble. They slide off the rig and into the sea.

**Turn the page.**

Hawkgirl lands on the deck as the rig workers cheer. She looks around.

"Where's Aquaman?" she asks.

"Aquaman isn't here," the foreman replies.

"What? Where did he go?" Hawkgirl asks.

The workers look confused. "Uh . . . he was never here," someone says.

"Oh no! I went to the wrong oil rig!" Hawkgirl realizes.

"There are many offshore platforms along the coast. But we're glad you came to ours," the foreman says. "Thank you, Hawkgirl!"

The rest of the workers clap and cheer again.

Hawkgirl gives them a nod. Then she leaps into the sky to continue her mission to find Aquaman.

"I suppose I'll consider this a warm-up," the hero mutters.

Turn to page 96.

"Let the tablet go!" Aquaman tells Martian Manhunter as the tablet sinks. "I can have one of my sea subjects get it later!"

Manhunter decides this is a good idea. He turns away from the tablet and helps Aquaman protect Manta's men from the monsters. But a swarm of whirling worms comes right after him!

In his monster form, the Martian Manhunter is four times the size of the creatures. But the worms do not seem to care. They bounce off his lobster-like upper body and keep coming back. He swipes his spiked serpent tail and snaps his claws.

Green Lantern bashes the creatures with the green energy fist holding Black Manta. The villain is knocked around inside the energy construct.

"I will not be treated like this!" shouts Black Manta.

Furious, he blasts his eye beams at the energy fist holding him. But Green Lantern simply uses his mental willpower to tighten his grip.

**Turn the page.**

Aquaman glances back at Manta's men. Even though he's fighting off the monster attacks, the criminals are still in danger. They're too deep in the ocean for them to swim to the surface. Aquaman calls upon his sea subjects to rescue the helpless henchmen.

Dolphins, sea turtles, and giant manta rays lift them upward. Aquaman protects them all. He beats back the worm creatures with his trident.

But something else rises from the gloom below.

"What in the Seven Seas is that?" Aquaman exclaims.

The monster looks like an enormous starfish. It's bigger than a whale. And it's covered with spikes that crackle with bioelectricity.

Suddenly the creature shoots bolts of electricity at the worm monsters. The stunned worms fall toward the starfish's waiting mouth.

**CRUUUNCH!**

The starfish cracks their shells and gobbles them up. Then it moves toward the humans.

"These aren't just monsters. They're part of a food chain," Aquaman realizes.

"Well, I sure don't want to be on the menu," Green Lantern mutters.

"I can take care of this. I will change my density so that its bioelectricity cannot harm me," Martian Manhunter says.

He switches from his Martian monster shape back to humanoid form, but he keeps his gigantic size. He reaches out.

The starfish erupts with lightning as soon as Manhunter grabs one of its limbs. Brilliant bolts of energy cover the pair like a sizzling spider web.

## *CRAAAAKKKKLLL! ZZZZAAAAT!*

The monster twists violently, trying to break the Martian Manhunter's hold.

Manhunter grows bigger and bigger until the starfish fits into the palm of his hand. He closes his fist around the creature. Bolts of bioelectricity stab out between Manhunter's giant fingers.

**Turn to page 99.**

High up in the Batplane, Batman can see the monsters swarming the harbor. He also sees Wonder Woman atop the lighthouse tower. She's fighting off creatures crawling up its sides.

Batman realizes that Wonder Woman is outnumbered. Even with her Amazon abilities, she can't battle all those monsters at once.

The Dark Knight makes his decision.

"Flash, Wonder Woman needs my help. I'm heading for the harbor," Batman says over the comm device. Then he signals Wonder Woman. "I'm on my way."

"Thanks. If you take care of the monsters on the ground, I can concentrate on the ones attacking this lighthouse. Divide and conquer," Wonder Woman replies.

Batman swoops over the herd of spider-rhino creatures thundering toward the harbor. He presses a button on the control panel. A series of Bat-grenades drops from the Batplane.

*BOOOMF! BOOOMF!*

**Turn the page.**

The Bat-grenades release a powerful knockout gas. Billowing clouds cover the monsters.

Next, the Dark Knight sets his attention on iguana monsters charging through the harbor.

Batman drops a net. It closes around the creatures, and he lifts them into the air. They whip their bodies and tails against the net. The Batplane rocks violently from side to side.

Inside the cockpit, alarms blare. The aircraft is starting to fall. Batman struggles to turn the Batplane toward the cloud of Bat-gas still on the ground. If he can reach it, the gas will knock out the squirming monsters.

"All I need is a few more seconds," he says as he fights for control. "If I don't crash first."

The Batplane disappears into the cloud of knockout gas. When it comes out, the net is not attached anymore.

"It's nap time for those monsters," Batman tells Wonder Woman over the comm. "That should take the pressure off you."

"Thanks, Batman. With the monsters on the ground taken care of, I can deal with the rest," Wonder Woman replies.

She twirls a beast over her head with her golden lasso. Then she swings the monster into others crawling up the side of the lighthouse.

**THWAAAK! THWAAAK!**

They tumble into the water below. She releases the monster from her lasso, and it splashes down into the sea. But more monsters crawl up to take their place.

"These things just don't know when to stop," Wonder Woman says. "Neither do I."

Wonder Woman uses her lasso to swing off the top of the tower. She lands on the back of a lizard creature crawling up. She wraps her lasso around its neck like a wild mustang. Then she turns it around and rides it down the side of the lighthouse.

The hero charges through the climbing monsters.

**Turn to page 103.**

Hawkgirl flies higher and higher. She flies just below a layer of clouds as she searches for the right oil rig with her super-keen vision.

But that's not the only thing she's watching for. She's also on the lookout for any flying creatures that might be hiding in the clouds. She could be ambushed at any moment. If she were a sky monster, that's what she would do.

Hawkgirl grips her battle mace. Her nerves are stretched tight.

Hawkgirl's instincts are correct. Suddenly an enormous shape plunges out of the clouds and rushes past her. She catches a glimpse of bat wings and a serpent body, plus a familiar orange-and-green uniform.

"Aquaman?!" Hawkgirl gasps.

Her teammate is riding on the back of a monster like a bucking bronco.

"Who knew a sea serpent could flyyyy?" Aquaman shouts as the monster carries him down. Then up. And then down again.

Hawkgirl dives and smacks the flying serpent with her battle mace.

**WHAAAAP!**

The creature goes limp and drops through the sky. Aquaman jumps from its back. He starts to fall toward the ocean.

"I've got you!" Hawkgirl yells.

She swoops in and catches the Sea King.

"Thanks," Aquaman says. "Manhunter, Green Lantern, and I were battling sea monsters. It turns out the one I was fighting could fly."

"I brought the tablet. It's in my belt, but I can't reach it. My hands are a bit full," Hawkgirl says. She holds Aquaman in one arm and grips her mace club in her other hand.

Aquaman pulls the artifact from Hawkgirl's belt. He works on interpreting the Atlantean text as Hawkgirl looks for a dry place to land. By the time she perches on top of an oil rig, Aquaman has an answer.

**Turn the page.**

"These markings are like a formula," Aquaman says. "And it involves high amounts of energy. If Black Manta's eye beams opened the portal, maybe the energy of your mace could close it."

"It's still open?" Hawkgirl says. "But I've been carrying that around in my belt! What are we waiting for? Let's close it!"

Aquaman holds out the tablet, and Hawkgirl strikes it with her energized mace club.

**KABLAAAM!**

Energy erupts in a burst of brilliant light. Then the artifact turns red-hot and starts to melt in Aquaman's hands. He drops it into the sea.

"I guess your mace energy caused it to self-destruct," Aquaman says.

"At least no more monsters will come through," Hawkgirl adds. "Now, let's go take care of the ones that are left."

### THE END

To follow another path, turn to page 12.

Green Lantern floats over to Martian Manhunter. He brings his energy fist holding Black Manta next to his teammate's enormous fist holding the starfish monster.

"OK, your fish is bigger than my fish," Green Lantern admits with a smile.

One of Black Manta's arms still sticks out from Green Lantern's energy fist like a stiff toothpick. Up until now, the villain has been furious at having to be in the embarrassing position.

But now he realizes that it's an advantage. His arm is the only part of his body not trapped inside the power ring construct. And it's also the part of his undersea armor that has a wrist gauntlet weapon.

Black Manta fires an energy blast from his gauntlet. It hits the bioelectric energy sparking out of Martian Manhunter's fist.

The result is explosive.

*BWAAAAAMM!*

**Turn the page.**

Green Lantern and Martian Manhunter are thrown back by the extreme eruption of energy. Even Manhunter's giant size can't protect him from the blast. The underwater shock wave catches him and tosses him. But he hangs onto the starfish monster.

The explosion takes Green Lantern by surprise, and the hero's concentration breaks for a second. That's all it takes for his power ring construct to waver. Black Manta slips free.

The villain fires energy blasts from his eye lenses. He doesn't have a target. He's just using the blasts to hide his escape.

But Black Manta can't fool the Sea King.

"Oh, no you don't," Aquaman says and quickly snags his foe on the tip of his trident.

Together the super heroes head back to the surface with the captured villain.

Turn to page 102.

Manta's men are already at the surface, resting on the backs of Aquaman's sea subjects. As soon as the henchmen see their boss, they swim over.

"You abandoned us to monsters!" they yell.

They try to attack Black Manta, but Green Lantern forms a net of green energy. He hauls the minions out of the water like fish from the sea.

"Aquaman, I would be grateful if you sent one of your sea subjects to retrieve the portal tablet. I would like to send this annoying creature back where it came from," Martian Manhunter says.

The starfish monster still wriggles in his giant hand. It keeps throwing out bolts of bioelectricity.

"I'll take care of it personally," the Sea King says. "But first . . ."

He flings Black Manta from his trident. Manhunter catches the villain in his other huge hand.

Aquaman smiles. "Hold onto this for me."

**THE END**

To follow another path, turn to page 12.

Wonder Woman jumps off the lizard's back when she reaches the ground. She releases it from her lasso and uses her amazing Amazon strength to lift the monster off its feet. She tosses it at the creatures swarming nearby. They tumble into each other and are knocked out cold.

"Are there any more?" Wonder Woman asks as she looks around.

A lizard monster staggers up out of the water and stumbles toward the super hero. It hisses when it sees her.

"I see you still have some fight left in you," Wonder Woman says. She steps toward the creature, clanking her Amazon bracelets together.

The large lizard shakes its head at the sharp sound. It lets out another angry hiss and charges.

Wonder Woman dodges the attack. She grabs the creature's tail and flips the beast onto its back. It thrashes violently, but Wonder Woman digs her heels into the ground and holds on tight.

"I feel like an alligator wrestler!" she says.

**Turn the page.**

The creature squirms and rolls. But it starts to slow down. Then it stops completely.

"Giving up so soon?" Wonder Woman asks. She lets go of its tail.

Immediately the beast jumps to its feet. It lunges at her.

Wonder Woman leaps to the side to avoid getting trampled. "Ugh, I've been tricked by a giant lizard. I'm never going to live this down," she mutters. "But there's a way to make up for my mistake."

Wonder Woman leaps high into the air. As she comes down, she slams both fists into the beast.

**WHAAACK!**

The creature is knocked out cold.

Wonder Woman stands in the middle of a mass of defeated monsters as Batman lands the Batplane nearby. She jumps over the unconscious creatures to join him.

"These things aren't going to stay asleep forever," Batman says, climbing out of the cockpit. "We need something to hold them."

"There are so many. There isn't a cage big enough!" Wonder Woman says.

"Maybe not, but a net will do. How are your weaving skills?" Batman asks. He points to huge spools of steel cable waiting to be loaded onto a cargo ship.

"It will be just like when I was a child making fishing nets," Wonder Woman says.

As she lifts two heavy spools and gets to work, The Flash zooms up. He joins his teammates.

"I took care of the volcano. Can I help here?" The Flash asks.

"That depends," Wonder Woman says. She holds up a spool. "How good are you at weaving?"

**THE END**

To follow another path, turn to page 12.

# AUTHOR

Laurie S. Sutton has read comics since she was a kid. She grew up to become an editor for Marvel, DC Comics, Starblaze, and Tekno Comics. She has written Adam Strange for DC, Star Trek: Voyager for Marvel, plus Star Trek: Deep Space Nine and Witch Hunter for Malibu Comics. There are long boxes of comics in her closet where there should be clothing and shoes. Laurie has lived all over the world, and currently resides in Florida.

# ILLUSTRATOR

Erik Doescher is a concept artist for Gearbox Software and a professional illustrator. He attended the School of Visual Arts in New York City and has freelanced for DC Comics for almost twenty years, in addition to many other licensed properties. He lives in Texas with his wife, five kids, two cats, and two fish.

# GLOSSARY

**alloy** (AL-oi)—a substance made of two or more metals

**artifact** (AR-tuh-fakt)—an object used in the past that was made by people

**bioelectricity** (buy-oh-ih-lek-TRIS-ih-tee)—electricity made by a living thing

**cybernetic** (sy-buhr-NET-ik)—something artificial and mechanical that is attached to a living thing

**horde** (HAWRD)—a very large group

**kraken** (KRAH-kuhn)—a gigantic sea monster from Norwegian myths

**minion** (MIN-yuhn)—someone who obeys the orders of a leader and isn't powerful or important

**optic** (OP-tik)—having to do with eyes; an optic blast is a burst of power from the eyes

**phase** (FEYZ)—to change the makeup of something solid so that things can pass through it

**portal** (POUR-tuhl)—an entrance or doorway, especially one that's very large and impressive

**sonar** (SOH-nar)—a device or method that uses sound waves to find objects; sonar is especially used to find objects underwater

**sonic** (SON-ik)—having to do with sound waves

**telepathy** (te-LEH-puh-thee)—the ability to communicate between minds without speaking or using signals

# BLACK MANTA

**Real Name:**
Unknown

**Occupation:**
Assassin and
Treasure Hunter

**Height:**
6 feet 4 inches

**Weight:**
250 pounds

**Eyes:**
Brown

**Hair:**
Brown

Before Black Manta became a super-villain, he was a young boy with a severe illness. His only comfort . . . the sea. One day while playing in the ocean, he was kidnapped and imprisoned on a ship. For years, the boy endured harsh treatment by his captors. Then he spotted hope on the horizon—Aquaman. He called out for help, but the Sea King did not hear him. At that moment the boy vowed revenge against Aquaman. After escaping from the ship, he designed a high-tech diving suit and took the name Black Manta, devil of the deep.

- Black Manta modeled his suit after real-life sea creatures called manta rays. The suit allows the super-villain to breathe underwater. It's also equipped with a variety of gadgets, including jet boots, mini torpedoes, and wrist gauntlets. Most powerful of all are the deadly optic beams Black Manta can shoot through the two large eye lenses on his helmet.

- Although Black Manta can swim at super-speed thanks to his suit, the villain often travels in the Manta Ship. This manta-ray shaped vessel can fly through the air, but it's also a swift submarine.

- Black Manta has two goals— destroy Aquaman and rule the seas. Fueled by extreme rage, he will stop at nothing to achieve these evil objectives.